Beautifully Made

Sonje D. Jack

Dedication

This book was written for any woman that has felt less than. Less than beautiful, less than worthy. Each day we wake up is another day that we could be judged or put down, but its for us to take a stand and know that we are all beautifully made. Beauty is skin deep. Beauty is in our blood.

CONTENTS

Acknowledgements

First and foremost, I'd like to thank God for allowing me to build up the courage to write this. To my sister for inspiring me to continue to write. To Axel my fiancé thank you for listening to me and keeping me motivated daily and supporting me no matter how wild the decision. My children and my family I love you all.

ONE

The End.

So, here we are. You think your life is over, right? We're here at the end. The last straw. The final break. The last insult, the last heartbreak, the last negative test, the last loss. Just the last. The end. But is it the end? The end of what? The end of what you thought was going to happen. Because the only real end is "THE END." So, ask yourself. I am serious, ask yourself what was it the end of? If you can ask yourself, that means you are living which means its not the end. Until the clock stops it will never be the end. Each morning wake up with a new mind. Its not the end, it is in the past. Take a rest today. Tomorrow we will start the beginning, we're way too far from the end.

TWO

Am I Worthy?

Am I worthy? Yes, I am. Yes, I am.
There's no way around it so if you're
reading this, this is self-affirmation. I Am
worthy. Of love, respect, a fair chance, joy,
peace, happiness. I am worthy of
forgiveness for the mistakes I've made in
the past. I'm worthy regardless of the path
life took me on, no matter how society
views me. If God said I was beautifully and
wonderfully made, why wouldn't I be
worthy? I don't want to be praised, no, just
appreciated. And I am worthy of that.

THREE

A Mothers Worry.

The children are good. They're getting big you know. Growing, learning. Exploring. Eventually they won't need me anymore. And that is my fear. I know the world, and its so hard. It is tough and its dark and I want to protect them every step of the way, but I know I won't. I'm rambling yes, but I'm worried. I'm worried the world will take them out because its so tough. I'm worried I wont be around to save them from the bullies. I'm worried my child might not wake up in the morning or make it home safe. I'm worried. I'm worried.

FOUR

A Mothers Beauty.

The scars and the stretch marks do not make you who you are. Imagine growing a human, multiple humans, in a body you never thought could. The beauty- The body we've taught ourselves to hate made something so beautiful so, aren't we? I mean you carry the weight of the world while giving birth to it. Mother you are beautiful. Just so beautiful.

Five

A Mothers Prayer.

Dear God, you know I'm trying my best. But somedays my best won't be enough so I'm asking you to please watch over my children. I can't see all evil so protect them from the evils that are present and the ones that hide. Keep them happy and healthy and safe. I pray my children always have a safe environment to thrive and grow. Provide for them when I cannot God. They are the head and not the tail, above and not beneath. They are successful, and I will forever be proud of the people they are and the people they'll become. Help me guide them and raise them the right way. Amen.

SIX

But Now What?

I can't relate. I can't relate to my friends sometimes. Some are married some have kids, some are single. some know what they're doing with their lives and I'm stuck asking, but now what? I'm at the point where all doors seem open for everyone else and not me. I'm stuck, I'm lost, now what? But now what do I do? But now what do I say to them? To her, to him? But now what?

Seven

Single FOREVER?

So, your heart was broken right?
And now absolutely no one in the world is
going to want you because? You're only as
single as you choose to be, and not the way
you are thinking. How can you be single
when you are loving yourself? Loving your
life? Loving your faith? You could not be
single but building a relationship with
yourself, its impossible. The relationship
between you and you is so important it
trumps all other relationships. Until you love
yourself first, you'll never really be in a
relationship. You'll know your worth and
understand it as well. Once you do then
you'll be truly ready for relationships.

Eight

God YOU There?

      Sometimes I question if God is even
there. I feel horrible saying that because how
can you pray to someone you don't always
believe. Its natural. It's normal. The world
tends to get so gray we forget the beautiful
vivid colors. Tend to forget how beautiful
and precious we are so we question God are
you there? You can't be if its this bad, if I'm
losing all hope. My back is against the wall.
I've been praying for this, are you listening?
Are you there?

But then the sun shines and the day is bright,
and my skin is glowing, and I feel like today
I can. It's at that moment I ask again God
are you there? Is this you?

Nine

I AM....

    I am tired. That's what we say more than anything. I'm fine. I'm okay. I'm doing well. I'm surviving. Without noticing those are the words we speak over our lives. Every single day, every single time you say "I'm fine" that's exactly all you are, is fine. Once we change the way we speak about ourselves well start to see the change. I am doing very great, I am blessed thank you, I am wise, I am beautiful, I am enough. I am stronger than the situation and tougher than the outcome. I am beautifully made.

Ten

The Beginning

We've reached your beginning. It seems to have come at the end, but it's the end of the chapter not the book. Funny how things work, for something to begin something must end. It seems so quick sometimes but that how it goes. Life wont wait but it does not mean you cannot take a break. You start when you are ready but in the meantime rest. Pray, meditate, cry but be joyful, thankful, because the beginning is here and its ready whenever you are. I'm excited for this, for your journey, for our journey. I'm hopeful and I know our beginning is here. Its your time. Its my time.

The Beginning.

Something For You,

Here is a 14-day guide on things to write *about*. For each sentence starter write the first thing that comes to mind. No matter how positive or negative write your feelings down. Somethings are better said out loud but in a private place, use it to reflect but not dwell. Instead as a stepping block and a resource to look back on to show yourself how much you have grown. We owe ourselves the best care and being honest with "me" is step one. There are no lines, fill the page this is for you. I'm so proud of your beginning, and always know you are beautifully made.

Day 1: Yes I Can...

Day 2: It Bothers Me That….

Day 3: Things About Me I've Learned to Love….

Day 4: Dear God…..

Day 5: I believe I will…

Day 6: Doubts/Fears?

Day 7: Letter To The Younger Me.

Day 8: I'm Going to Try….

Day 9: To The Ones I Lost,

Day 10: I Break ALL Generational Curses
On Myself, Things Said By....

Day 11: I forgive Myself....

Day 12: I Forgive…

Day 13: I Am Healing From…

Day 14: I Have Healed From…

Finally, before we rest, I am Beautiful Because.....

About The Author

After having my son at 19 and my daughter at 21 I asked myself so many hard questions. I didn't think I was beautiful or worthy of love. I lost myself and tried to fine me in so many wrong places. Its so easy to believe the negative things said about you but its my choice to believe it as well.

I started speaking positive words over my negative situations. I started to learn that because it was a bad day didn't mean it was a bad life. I saw that I was beautifully made, and if babies don't worry about what they look like then why should I? I want to live free of self-hate and worry that I'm fitting a nonexistent mold. I am the way I am supposed to be. I am beautifully made. In Gods image all the same. Beautiful.

Made in the USA
Middletown, DE
22 May 2021